The Adventures of Bumber the Umbrella

A Complete Me Book

By Elki Powers

I began writing and illustrating this book many years ago. Now, I need your help. The first 12 pages are complete and should get your imagination started. For the end of the book, grab your markers and complete the rest. You may want to use sheets of paper instead of drawing inside the book, so others can have fun, too. You can email pictures of your completed drawings to info@virtualbookworm.com.

"The Adventures of Bumber the Umbrella," by Elki Powers. ISBN 978-1-63868-081-9 (softcover).

Published 2022 by Virtualbookworm.com Publishing, P.O.Box 9949, College Station, TX, 77842, US.

Bumber was an umbrella.

Bumber lived in a trunk.

Bumber was
in the trunk
most of the
time.

But there were many days that
he came out of the trunk.....

..... and went out of
the house...

....where it was <u>ALWAYS</u> raining.

The rain went

blump

blump

blump !!

...right on top of Bumber.

At first it was always fun.

Then, it was not so funny.

THEN, it was <u>un</u>-fun!

..... and Bumber wanted to run home.

But Bumber could not run home when the rain was un-funny because.......

....there was always someone under him.

Sometimes Mister Fuddle was
            under Bumber.....

Sometimes it was Missus Fuddle....

And sometimes it was
     Buddy Fuddle.

One day Buddy Fuddle put Bumber into his trunk when he was still wet....

...and Bumber got a cold and a big red nose !!

and was very UNHAPPY.

So Mister Fuddle took
Bumber into the sun.

Now Bumber had NEVER seen the sun. He had always
seen outside like this...

And never like this...

First, he was afraid, because it was NEW.

Then he was puzzled, because it was WRONG.

Then he felt the warm sun, and was not afraid or puzzled.

After a while, Bumber was dry and his nose was not so red. Then he was not even a little afraid … but he was still a little puzzled.

So the Fuddle family let Bumber live on top of his trunk, just under a window.

Finally, Bumber was not puzzled - not even a little bit.

He saw that outside was not always like this ... (rainy)

But sometimes like this ... (sunny)

Or like this .... (gray)

Or like this ... (night)

And Bumber was very happy!